Let's Go CAMPING with Mr. Sillypants

M·K· BROWN

Crown Publishers, Inc., New York

For Robbie Barrows, Katie Booth,
Thomas Oliver, Lucas B. Sharp,
and Megan Thorpe

CROWN is a trademark of Crown Publishers, Inc.

Manufactured in Mexico

Library of Congress Cataloging-in-Publication Data
Brown, M. K. (Mary K.) Let's go camping with Mr. Sillypants / by M. K. Brown
p.   cm.
Sequel to: Let's go swimming with Mr. Sillypants. Summary: When Mr. Sillypants gets lost on a camping trip, he has a dream about "The Three Bears." [1. Camping—Fiction. 2. Dreams—Fiction. 3. Humorous stories.] I. Title. PZ7.B81616Le 1995 [E]—dc20   94-15991

ISBN 0-517-59773-X (trade)
0-517-59774-8 (lib. bdg.)
10 9 8 7 6 5 4 3 2 1

First Edition

This is the morning of the big camping trip.
Too bad Mr. Sillypants overslept.

Ten-thirty!

And what a charming cottage.
I wonder who lives here.

Nothing but trees.

And now it's really getting dark.

And it was.